Dear Parents:

Congratulations! Your child is taking the first steps on an exciting journey. The destination? Independent reading!

STEP INTO READING® will help your child get there. The program offers five steps to reading success. Each step includes fun stories and colorful art or photographs. In addition to original fiction and books with favorite characters, there are Step into Reading Non-Fiction Readers, Phonics Readers and Boxed Sets, Sticker Readers, and Comic Readers—a complete literacy program with something to interest every child.

Learning to Read, Step by Step!

Ready to Read   **Preschool–Kindergarten**
• big type and easy words • rhyme and rhythm • picture clues
For children who know the alphabet and are eager to begin reading.

Reading with Help   **Preschool–Grade 1**
• basic vocabulary • short sentences • simple stories
For children who recognize familiar words and sound out new words with help.

Reading on Your Own   **Grades 1–3**
• engaging characters • easy-to-follow plots • popular topics
For children who are ready to read on their own.

Reading Paragraphs   **Grades 2–3**
• challenging vocabulary • short paragraphs • exciting stories
For newly independent readers who read simple sentences with confidence.

Ready for Chapters   **Grades 2–4**
• chapters • longer paragraphs • full-color art
For children who want to take the plunge into chapter books but still like colorful pictures.

STEP INTO READING® is designed to give every child a successful reading experience. The grade levels are only guides; children will progress through the steps at their own speed, developing confidence in their reading.

Remember, a lifetime love of reading starts with a single step!

For Hillary —C.C.
For my mother, the superhero
of my every day —P.Ø.

Copyright © 2017 DC Comics. DC SUPER HERO GIRLS and all
related characters and elements © & ™ DC Comics and Warner Bros.
Entertainment Inc. WB SHIELD: ™ & © WBEI. (s17)
RHUS39299

Visit us on the Web!
StepIntoReading.com
randomhousekids.com
dcsuperherogirls.com
dckids.com

Educators and librarians, for a variety of teaching tools, visit us at RHTeachersLibrarians.com

ISBN 978-1-5247-6606-1 (trade) — ISBN 978-1-5247-6607-8 (lib. bdg.)
ISBN 978-1-5247-6608-5 (ebook)

Printed in the United States of America

10 9 8 7 6 5 4 3 2 1

DC SuperHero Girls™

Showdown in Space!

by Courtney Carbone
illustrated by Pernille Ørum

Random House 🏠 New York

"Wow," said Wonder Woman.

"Look at that ceiling!"

"The dome protects us

from asteroids and other threats,"

the president said.

Whoosh!

Just then, Speed Queen zipped by,
almost crashing into the heroes.
Stompa and Artemiz followed.

They went to a rival school
on the planet Apokolips.
"Move it!" Speed Queen said,
pushing past the heroes.

The heroes found seats
beside students from
Korugar Academy,
another rival school.

One of the students, Blackfire,
ignored the heroes.
But two others,
Mongal and Bleez,
greeted them.

"Have you done this before?"
Wonder Woman asked.

"Not exactly," Mongal replied.

"My whole family is warlike,
especially my brother, Mongul.
They believe in fighting."

The Model UP president
warmly welcomed the heroes
to the space station.
Thousands of stars twinkled
through the clear dome overhead.

It was time for the yearly
Model United Planets meeting.
Wonder Woman, Supergirl,
and Starfire were excited
to represent Super Hero High!

"So does ours," Starfire said,

looking at Blackfire.

Mongal was confused.

"We're sisters," Starfire explained.

"Unfortunately," Blackfire sighed.

The Model UP president
took the stage.
"Welcome," she began.
"Model United Planets is
all about working together—"

Suddenly, an alarm sounded!
Warning lights flashed
in the auditorium.

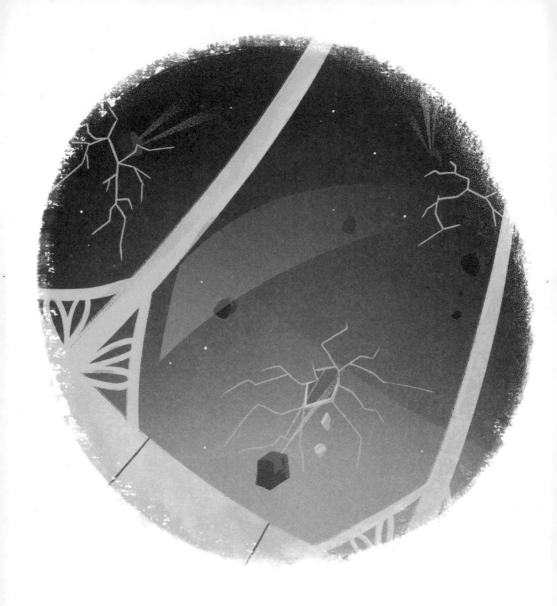

Clink! Clink! Clink! CRASH!

Asteroids began smashing

into the dome!

"This isn't a drill!"

Wonder Woman shouted.

"Let's go, girls!"

Cracks crept up the walls
as more asteroids smashed
the dome.
A heavy column collapsed.
Wonder Woman caught it!

"This isn't natural," Starfire said.

"It's an attack!"

Supergirl flew up and
used her super-strength
to support the collapsing dome.

Supergirl saw the attacker.
"Mongal," she said, "I think someone
stole your fashion sense."

Mongal looked up.

"It's my little brother!" she growled.

"Mongul, what are you doing?"

"I'm just having fun," he laughed.

"Then I'm telling Dad
you're learning about peace and
teamwork. He won't like that!"
Just then, an asteroid smashed
Mongul against the dome.

The dome finally broke!
Mongul fell through it,
and the air began to escape!

"We've got to plug that hole!"
Wonder Woman shouted.
"I can help!" cried Bleez.
She used her power ring
to create a temporary force field.

Starfire and Blackfire teamed up
to weld the ceiling back together
with their star bolt powers.

Supergirl used her heat vision
to seal the final cracks.
Everyone was safe again!

Supergirl and Bleez
high-fived.

Blackfire fist-bumped Starfire.

"Good work, sis," she said.

Even Stompa couldn't resist
lending a foot—a big one,
right on Mongul's chest!

"I guess you weren't joking
about your warlike family,"
Wonder Woman said to Mongal.
"Unfortunately, no," Mongal replied.
"But Mongul will be in so much
trouble when he gets home."

"On the side that is up,"
Starfire said to Blackfire,
"*our* rivalry is not so bad."
Blackfire nodded and patted
her sister on the back.

"What now?" Supergirl asked.

The president smiled and said,

"Hero cake for everyone!"